KENJU'S FOREST

For Meggan

COLLINS PUBLISHERS AUSTRALIA

First published in 1989 by William Collins Pty Ltd,
55 Clarence Street, Sydney, NSW 2000
in association with Anne Ingram Books
First published in paperback 1990
Illustrations copyright: © Junko Morimoto 1989

Typeset by FullStop in Optima
Produced by Mandarin Offset, Hong Kong

National Library of Australia
Cataloguing-in-Publication data:

Kenju's forest.

ISBN 0 7322 4894 9. (hardback)
ISBN 0 7322 7358 7. (paperback)

I. Morimoto, Junko, 1932-   . II. Miyazawa, Kenji,
1896-1933.

895.6'3'4

Adaptation copyright: © Helen Smith 1989
Editor: Anne Bower Ingram

KENJU'S FOREST

Junko Morimoto

COLLINS PUBLISHERS AUSTRALIA
in association with
ANNE INGRAM BOOKS

Kenju loved to wander along the paths that lay between the rice fields. He would reach up to the sky and laugh aloud.

The birds sang and the trees danced in the wind — how wonderful it all was.

Everyone in the village laughed at Kenju, but this did not spoil his happiness.

One day Kenju came running across the field to his family. The last frost had passed and they were busy preparing for spring.

"Mother! Mother!" he called, even more excited than usual. "Would you buy me lots of cedar trees to plant in our empty field behind the house?"

His family stopped work and looked up at Kenju, who waited, a small smile trembling on his lips.

At last his Father spoke, "Kenju is a good boy. He has never asked for anything and that field has been empty for so long. Go and buy him the seedlings," he said, turning to Kenju's brother.

The next morning Kenju was up with the sun. It was a shining winter's day.

Kenju listened carefully to his brother's instructions; he wanted to do everything just right. He had dreamt about his trees, standing like soldiers in long straight rows.

They had been working steadily when suddenly Heiji appeared. He owned the farm next door but spent most of his time in the village.

"If your stupid trees do grow, they will block out my sun!" Heiji barked.

Kenju froze, for Heiji had always frightened him. Luckily, his brother was nearby. He straightened up and, glaring at Heiji, said, "Good morning to you, Heiji! Aren't you working today?"

Heiji just grunted and went back to town.

It seemed to take forever for the seedlings to grow. The whole village laughed at Kenju. They had all told him so.

Nevertheless, Kenju was proud of his trees. He would stand for hours on the edge of the field admiring them.

One day the villagers decided to play a joke on Kenju.

"It's about time you pruned your trees, young Kenju. All those lower branches should be lopped off," advised one of the farmers, looking very serious.

He thanked the farmer for this advice, then set off to find his axe.

Kenju pruned his treasured cedars, branch after branch.

It was nearly dusk when he stopped and looked up. He had done exactly as the farmer had told him, but it saddened him to see all the branches lying on the ground.

Just then his brother arrived. He patted Kenju warmly on the shoulder, "Don't worry young brother. Come on, let's collect all these branches and we'll build a big bonfire."

The next day a new sound filled the air. It floated across the field and into the hut.

Kenju stopped and listened. It was a happy sound which filled the air and brought a smile to his face.

Suddenly, realising where the sound had come from, Kenju leapt to his feet and ran out of the hut.

Kenju followed the sound. He stopped at the edge of
the field, and stared.

Children, lots and lots of children, great lines of children,
were marching, weaving their way through the rows of trees.

Their laughter and singing sent all the birds flying into the air.

In the background, Kenju watched and listened. His joy burst out and melted into the trees.

The forest had become a magical playground for all the village children. It was only when the leaves dripped with rain that the forest was still and rested.

On these days Kenju could be seen standing quietly among the trees, the rain running gently down his face.

"On guard again today, Kenju?" someone would ask as they hurried by.

Although Kenju's trees sheltered Heiji's field from the harsh winds, Heiji still hated the forest.

One morning he caught Kenju alone. "Cut them down! Cut them down!" Heiji screamed over and over again.

Kenju's eyes filled with tears, he turned to face Heiji, "No, I won't," he quietly replied.

Enraged, Heiji stormed off, muttering loudly as he went.

The season that followed was severe. The winds blew stronger and colder, the snow lay deeper on the ground than even the oldest in the village could remember.

During that terrible winter Kenju died. His trees stood still, silently wrapped in their icy grief.

Many others in the village, including Heiji, were taken with the same illness.

In time the village grew, and more children came to play
in Kenju's forest.

Thirty years passed.

The farms were all gone for the village had grown into a city.

In the middle of all the progress only Kenju's forest was unchanged.

At about this time, a famous professor returned to visit his old home. During a visit to the village school, he heard a sound of laughter. Looking up, he saw all the children playing in Kenju's forest.

"It's just the same, after all these years," he smiled. "Kenju's father has given the children the freedom of the forest," the Headmaster explained.

"Oh yes, I remember Kenju. We all thought that he was a little slow, but now I think that perhaps we were going too fast to see his world."

To this day, when you lie on the soft cool turf, the dark leaves will gently filter sunlight down upon your face. And like countless others, you will learn the secret of Kenju's happiness.